The Rescue Princesses

The Ice Diamond

More amazing
animal adventures!

The Secret Promise

The Wishing Pearl

The Moonlight Mystery

The Stolen Crystals

The Snow Jewel

The Magic Rings

The Lost Gold

The Shimmering Stone

The Silver Locket

The Rescue Princesses

The Ice Diamond

♥ PAULA HARRISON ♥

Scholastic Inc.

For Sarah and Elliot

ISBN 978-0-545-66164-5

Text copyright © 2014 by Paula Harrison
Interior Illustrations copyright © 2014 by Artful Doodlers

12 11 10 9 8 7 6 5 4 3   14 15 16 17 18 19/0

Printed in the U.S.A   40
First printing, April 2014

CHAPTER ONE

The Little Snow Leopard

Princess Maya leapt up the mountainside, jumping over rough stones and patches of star-shaped flowers. She climbed and climbed until she reached the huge flat rock called Ching-May Peak. Crawling onto the stone, she pushed her long black braid over her shoulder and gazed all around.

"I can see for miles. The palace looks so tiny!" she told Deena.

"How did you climb up so fast?" puffed

the rosy-cheeked lady below her. "You're like a mountain goat!"

Deena was a groom at the palace and, as well as caring for the horses, she also looked after the king's wildlife projects.

Maya turned to gaze at the view again while she was waiting for Deena to catch up. The gray, turreted palace that she lived in had shrunk to the size of a toy castle. All around it were the streets and houses of the city.

"I love it up here," she said, smiling. "I'm so glad you let me come with you."

"I'm happy to have your help. I want to write down all the wild animals we see so I can report back to the king." Deena took out a notepad and pencil. "He needs to know how the wildlife project's going."

"Do you think we'll see any snow leopards?" asked Maya.

"I really hope so," Deena replied.

Everyone in the kingdom of Lepari knew that the numbers of snow leopards had fallen over the last five years. There were very few of them left. The king, Maya's dad, had set up a nature project to help the endangered animals. It meant that no one was allowed to hurt them or to build houses on the mountain slopes where they lived. That way the leopards would be able to live in peace.

Maya tilted her head back to look at the tallest peak, which was glittering white with snow. A few weeks ago, the whole mountainside had been covered, but now it was springtime again!

"There are two mountain sheep," said Deena, scribbling on her notepad. "Can you see anything else, Maya?"

Maya turned her attention to the mountain slopes. Snow leopards were always well camouflaged. Their gray-and-white patterned coats were hard to spot against the rocks, but she thought she could see something moving.

"Look! There's a snow leopard!" Maya said excitedly. "Right next to those bushes."

The beautiful leopard had thick white fur speckled with dark rosettes. Maya watched it prowl across the mountain slope. It paused, crouching behind a boulder, its long tail flicking from side to side.

"Some people still call them by their old name: Spirits of the Mountain," said Deena softly. "I think it's because they're so graceful."

"It's amazing that they're such good climbers," said Maya.

Deena nodded. "This one's quite small, so it's probably a female. I wonder if it has any cubs."

Maya looked around eagerly. "I'd love to see some cubs!"

Deena wrote on her notepad. "Keep looking, then. Snow leopard dens are usually well hidden to keep the cubs safe."

Maya scanned the mountainside carefully. There! Something was moving among the rocks.

"Deena!" Maya tugged at her sleeve. "Is that a snow leopard cub?"

The white shape moved, and they saw a small furry head. Deena smiled broadly. "Yes, it is! It's a good thing I brought you along, Maya. Your eyes are much sharper than mine."

The larger snow leopard gave a low growl, and the cub bounded out from behind a rock. It gazed around and then scampered over to its mother, rubbing against her legs before leaping away.

Maya's heart thumped. "It's so cute," she whispered. "I wish we could go a little closer."

"It's best not to disturb them," Deena reminded her.

The mother leopard padded farther up the mountainside, and the cub followed her, bounding playfully from rock to rock.

"I'm going to call him Cloudtail," said Maya, "because his tail's exactly the same color as those clouds up there."

"That really fits him! Well, we'd better start climbing down again," said Deena, putting away her notepad. "The king wanted you back by ten o'clock to welcome all the royal visitors." She started clambering down the mountainside.

Maya sighed. "I wish we had more time." She took one last look at the little cub, who was running in and out of his mother's legs. Even from a distance, she

could see how soft his fur was and how his tail curled as he jumped. "See you soon, Cloudtail," she murmured. Then she hurried down the stony mountainside to catch up with Deena.

Together they made their way to the bottom and climbed into Deena's truck, which was parked at the side of a rough path.

"Do you know how many royal visitors are coming to stay?" Maya asked as Deena started the engine.

"A lot, I think," Deena replied. "Nobody outside of Lepari has seen our Spring Festival before. I think nearly one hundred people have accepted your father's royal invitation."

Maya swallowed. The thought of meeting all those people made her feel shy. "I was hoping that there wouldn't be too many guests coming."

Deena looked at her sympathetically. "There might be some princesses of your own age to play with."

Maya smiled and turned to watch the fields sweeping by the window. A few minutes later, they drove through the big stone arch that led to the palace, and stopped on the driveway.

"Later today, I'm traveling west to check on another wildlife area," Deena told her. "But I'll see you at the Spring Festival."

"Bye, Deena! Thanks for taking me to Ching-May Peak with you." Maya waved and then rushed off to the palace. She dashed around a corner, nearly running straight into a crowd of newly arrived kings and queens.

Her dad, King Ramesh, was standing on the steps in front of the gray stone palace wearing his emerald-green robes and golden crown. "Kings and Queens, Princes and Princesses," he said loudly. "Welcome to the kingdom of Lepari."

Queen Kala stepped forward carrying Maya's little brother, Ajay. "We're so pleased that you could all come to our Spring Festival."

The kings and queens clapped.

"But where is Princess Maya?" the king asked urgently. "She should be here by now. We need to introduce her to our guests."

Everyone looked around, murmuring in surprise, and Maya turned bright red. "I'm here," she said faintly.

"Ah, there you are, Maya." The king's frown cleared. "Come right to the front, please, and you can curtsy and say hello to all these visitors."

CHAPTER TWO

New Friends

Maya's feet felt heavy as she made her way to the front of the crowd. What if her curtsy went wrong or she fell over in front of everyone? She took a deep breath. She would just have to be brave.

Climbing up the steps, she stopped beside the king and turned to face the visitors. "Hello, everyone," she said quietly, and curtsied.

"Thank you, Maya!" The king beamed. "Now that we've done all that —"

"Don't forget me, dear Brother. I'm very important, after all." A thin man with a beak-like nose elbowed his way to the front. He turned to the visitors and swept a deep bow. "I am Duke Levon, the king's brother."

"I'm glad you could be here, Brother," said the king. "Now let's all go inside for refreshments. Our cook's made some wonderful cakes."

Murmuring in approval, the royal visitors made their way up the steps into the palace. The banquet hall was a long room with huge purple–and–gold pillars stretching up to the ceiling.

Many of the younger princes and princesses ran straight to the table in the middle, which was spread with delicious-looking cakes and glasses of sparkling lemonade. The grown-ups gazed toward the far side of the room at the magnificent throne, which had a large diamond fixed to the top.

"That diamond is enormous," said a gray-haired queen.

King Ramesh heard her. "It's also a very famous jewel. It was discovered by the first king of Lepari. The legend says that the Ice Diamond has great strength, and the king used its power to build the kingdom. It has been kept here ever since to give strength to each ruler."

"Why is it called the Ice Diamond?" asked the gray-haired queen.

"It was found stuck in a rock beneath the ice and snow at the very top of a mountain," explained the king.

Maya had known that the guests would be impressed by the Ice Diamond. Visitors always were because it was so large and glittered beautifully in the light. She helped herself to a piece of chocolate cake and began nibbling the sweet icing off the top as she gazed around at the guests.

She wanted to find some princesses her own age, but spotting them in the crowd was much harder than finding the cub on the mountainside that morning had been! She saw a group of princes crowding around a huge lemon cake. Then she caught sight of a younger princess with blond curls, but there were no girls her own age.

Maya brushed the cake crumbs off her hands and squeezed through the crowd to reach the door. Then she walked out of the hallway and down the front steps. After the busy, noisy banquet hall, it was nice to be outside in the empty garden. Suddenly, she heard the sound of voices and realized that it might not be empty after all.

The sound came from a small circle of trees that stood beyond the neat flower beds. Through a gap in the branches, Maya thought she saw two figures. Wondering who they were, she went closer.

A girl with tight red curls was marching up and down, only stopping to stare into the treetops. Another girl with short blond hair was watching her and frowning fiercely.

Maya crept a little closer and hid behind a tree trunk. What were they doing? They looked so serious that it couldn't be a game.

"You're looking in the wrong place. That wasn't where I threw it," said the blond-haired girl. "It was over here."

The red-haired girl put her hands on her hips. "How can you possibly *know* where it went, Rosalind? You threw it so wildly that it could be almost anywhere."

Rosalind's eyes flashed. "I'm the one who threw it, so of course I know. Look — there it is! Happy now?"

Maya looked at where she was pointing. A blue-and-white ball was stuck at the top of a tree. She recognized it as the one her little brother, Ajay, liked to play with.

"Come on! Let's shake the tree and get it down." The red-haired girl rushed over and shook the tree, showering them with leaves and twigs.

"Yuck! Stop it, Lottie!" Rosalind brushed the bits out of her hair. "That isn't working at all."

"Well, you think of something, then," said Lottie. "We've *got* to get the ball down. It probably belongs to that little prince, or maybe his sister with the long braid and the red dress."

Maya looked down at her red dress and smiled. They must mean her! She stepped out from behind the tree trunk, meaning to go and say hello, but her dress caught on a bramble. Bending down, she tried to unhook it.

Rosalind was staring so hard at the ball that she didn't notice Maya. "I'm going to climb right up the tree and get it. That's what any Rescue Princess would do!" She grabbed hold of the tree trunk and put her foot onto the lowest branch.

Maya freed her dress and straightened up. Had that girl just said *Rescue Princess*?

Lottie hadn't seen Maya, either. "Wait a sec! I'll give you a boost," she said, trying to push Rosalind up the tree.

"Ow! Stop it!" Rosalind wobbled wildly and then fell sideways with a shriek, knocking Lottie to the ground. The two girls lay there, groaning.

"Rosalind?" Lottie's voice was muffled. "You're squashing me."

Maya ran forward. "Oh, poor you! Are you both all right?"

Rosalind stood up, looking surprised. "Where did you come from? I didn't know there was anyone else out here."

"I . . ." Maya suddenly felt as if she shouldn't have been watching them. "I heard your voices, so I came to see who it was."

"So you were listening just now?" Rosalind frowned. "You shouldn't do that, you know."

"Rosy, don't be so suspicious!" Lottie sprang up, her green eyes sparkling. "Hello, I'm Lottie from the kingdom of Middingland. Don't mind Rosy. She just doesn't like anyone seeing her fall over."

"It's not that. I didn't know anyone was listening. We were talking about . . .

things." Rosalind gave Lottie a meaningful look.

Maya's cheeks flushed. "I didn't mean to listen. I'm Maya, and I live here at the palace. It's really nice to meet you." She stopped and bit her lip. She'd been hoping to meet some girls her own age and now she'd ruined it.

Rosalind's frown cleared, and she patted Maya's arm. "It's great to meet you, too! I'm Rosalind from the kingdom of Dalvia. I was really happy when my dad said we'd been invited to Lepari. I've never been anywhere with such big mountains. I wish I could go right up to the top of one!"

Maya laughed. "That would take days! Can I help you reach that ball?" She pulled herself up into the tree and knocked the ball down. "Have you seen any other princesses our age here?"

"The other princesses are mostly younger ones," said Lottie. "We were hoping to meet up with our friends Amina and Isabella, but they couldn't come."

Maya smiled. "Would you like me to show you around the palace? We could go and see the horses." She stopped, suddenly hearing a thin wailing noise.

"What's that?" asked Rosalind, her eyes widening. "It sounds like someone crying."

"I think it's my brother." Maya ran out of the trees. "Ajay, where are you? What's wrong?"

A little boy ran up and flung himself at Maya, tears on his cheeks. "Tilly's gone! Tilly's gone!"

"What happened?" Maya knelt down and hugged him.

"She jumped out of my arms." Ajay sniffed. "I didn't mean to let her go."

"Who's Tilly?" Lottie asked quickly.

"It's his rabbit," Maya explained. "She's a troublesome bunny. She often tries to escape from her run, and she isn't very easy to catch."

"Don't worry," Rosalind told Ajay. "Show us where she escaped, and we'll find her for you. We're great at helping animals!"

CHAPTER THREE

Pets and Surprises!

Ajay rushed across the garden with the three princesses close behind him. They ran through a tunnel of trees and stopped next to a pair of hutches in front of the stable yard.

"This is where we keep our rabbit and guinea pig," Maya explained to the other girls before turning to Ajay. "Which way did Tilly go after she jumped out of your arms?"

"I was over here." Ajay pointed to an

open hutch. "I tried to catch her, but she hopped away too fast." His little face crumpled. "I want Tilly back!"

Maya gave him another hug. "Don't worry. We'll find her." She was about to suggest that they should start searching in different places, but she realized in surprise that the others had already begun. Rosalind was peering under the hutches while Lottie was checking beneath the branches of a bush.

"There's nothing here. Have you found anything, Rosalind?" asked Lottie.

Rosalind shook her head. "There's no use looking for paw prints — we won't find any with the ground so dry."

"Let's take twenty paces in opposite directions and search again," said Lottie. "Ready?" She and Rosalind stood back to back. Then they walked away from each other, counting their steps.

Maya watched them in astonishment. These two girls had been arguing a minute ago, and now they looked as if they were princesses on a mission! She noticed that they had matching heart-shaped rings on their fingers, one sapphire and one ruby.

Hurrying forward, she joined in by looking behind a stack of hay bales. "Tilly?" she called. "Come out, bunny!"

Behind her she heard a soft echo. "Come out, bunny."

She turned around, wondering for a minute if someone was copying her. But she couldn't see anyone. Lottie and Rosalind were dashing over to the stable yard. Ajay was still standing by the open hutch, rubbing his eyes.

"Come out, bunny."

There it was again! Running around the hay bales, Maya found a girl crouching down next to a pile of flowerpots and gardening tools. She turned her head and smiled as Maya came closer. Her blond hair hung loosely around her pointed face. "There's a rabbit hiding down here," she explained. "But I think I can get her to come out."

Maya knelt down to look. "That's probably my brother's rabbit. I'm Maya, by the way."

"Hi." The other girl smiled again. "My name's Summer." There was a scrabbling noise behind a garden spade, and she turned her attention back to the rabbit. "Come on, bunny." She held out her hand.

Cautiously, Tilly poked her whiskery nose out to sniff Summer's fingers. Then she crept forward a little more, her dark brown eyes darting from Summer to Maya.

Lottie and Rosalind ran around the corner. "Did you find her?" asked Lottie breathlessly. "I can pick her up if you want."

"No, it's OK. I can do it." Summer quickly put a hand under the rabbit's tummy and scooped her out. Then she straightened up, stroking Tilly's fur gently.

"Ajay!" Maya called. "Look who we found!"

"Tilly!" Ajay dashed around the corner.

"Here you are!" Summer carefully handed the bunny to Ajay. "She's a cute rabbit."

"Thank you for finding her." Ajay smoothed Tilly's soft floppy ears. "I'm going to get her some treats." He carried the rabbit away.

"Oh, Summer! This is Lottie and

Rosalind," said Maya, realizing that she needed to introduce them all.

"You coaxed the rabbit out of there really easily," Lottie told Summer approvingly. "Do you like animals?"

"Yes, I have lots of pets at home, and I love wild animals, too." Summer shook back her hair. "I'm from the land of Mirrania. I bet you've heard of some of our wild animals — like koalas and kangaroos."

"We have some fantastic wildlife here, too," said Maya proudly. "I saw two snow leopards on the mountainside early this morning. One of the snow leopards was a little cub, and I've named him Cloudtail."

"Aw! You're so lucky!" cried Rosalind. "I would *love* to see a snow leopard cub."

"Me too!" Summer's eyes shone. "It would be like a dream come true."

An idea popped into Maya's head. "Maybe you can! I can take you up the mountain and show you the cub. It's perfectly safe as long as you don't get too close."

Lottie looked thoughtful. "Doesn't the Spring Festival start on Saturday? Because that would mean the next two days are totally free and we can do whatever we want."

"That's if the grown-ups let us," said Rosalind doubtfully.

"We should ask them right now," Lottie decided. "Why don't you try your dad first, Maya? If he says yes, then all the other kings and queens will have to agree."

"All right!" Maya beamed. "Let's go and ask."

Together, they ran back to the palace and found King Ramesh still talking in the banquet hall. The king's brother,

Duke Levon, was there, too, wearing a black velvet robe and a heavy gold chain that made him look even richer than the king.

"Dad?" said Maya. "Can I ask you something?" The other princesses crowded behind her.

The king turned around. "Yes, Maya, what is it?"

"Can I take these princesses up to Ching-May Peak tomorrow so that they can see the snow leopards?" Maya wound her braid around one finger. "They'd love to go."

"Go all the way up Ching-May Peak!" said Duke Levon sharply. "What nonsense! Little girls should stay inside the palace where they belong."

Maya wanted to tell her uncle that she'd been up the mountainside earlier that day with Deena, but she didn't dare.

He looked so fierce sometimes, with his dark eyes and sharp features.

The king silenced his brother with a look. "I'm afraid not, my dear," he told Maya. "At ten o'clock tomorrow morning, we'll begin a whole day of speeches leading up to the Spring Festival. We call it the Grand Assembly, and everyone will be there in full royal costume. "

Rosalind sighed loudly and folded her arms.

Maya blinked. A whole day of grown-ups talking! That would be awful. "But please, Dad —" she began.

"I'm sorry, Maya," said King Ramesh. "It's out of the question."

Maya's heart sank. She hated disappointing the other girls.

"Couldn't we go for a little while?" asked Lottie, but King Ramesh had turned to speak to some other guests and didn't hear her.

Maya led the other princesses over to a corner. "What are we going to do? A whole day of speeches sounds so boring, but my dad never changes his mind about anything."

"If the speeches don't start until ten o'clock, we could sneak out, see the snow leopards, and come back before they even realize we're gone," said Lottie.

"What if we're late?" asked Maya doubtfully. "We'll get in trouble."

Lottie and Rosalind exchanged glances. "There is a way we could sneak into the banquet hall without being seen, even in the middle of the speeches," said Rosalind.

"That's right," said Lottie. "We know ninja moves."

Summer's eyes widened. "Really?"

Rosalind nodded. "We have a book that helps us. . . ." She glanced around, checking that no one was listening. "Come to my room, and I'll show you."

They raced upstairs. Rosalind shut her bedroom door. Then, very carefully, she took a blue sweater out of her suitcase. Gently, she unfolded it to show them what lay inside — an old book with a black cover and golden letters on the front.

"This book . . ." Rosalind lowered her voice mysteriously, "is the secret *Book of Ninja!*"

"Wow! Is it very old?" asked Maya.

"It is." Rosalind nodded. "And every single ninja move ever invented is written down inside. It's been very useful."

"But what have you used it for?" asked Summer.

Lottie and Rosalind exchanged looks. "We said we'd keep all that a secret — remember?" said Lottie.

"I think we should tell them," said Rosalind. "They both love animals, and that's the most important part of being a *you know what*! Anyway, we need to teach them some ninja moves so that we can go to see the snow leopards."

Lottie nodded. "All right!" She turned to Maya and Summer. "We'll tell you our special secret as long as you promise not to tell anyone."

"I can keep a secret. Cross my heart!" Maya put her hand on her heart.

"Me too," said Summer.

"The secret is that Rosalind and I are Rescue Princesses!" Lottie told them. "We help animals in trouble no matter how dangerous it is. There are two other girls who are Rescue Princesses as well.

Together we've had lots of incredible adventures!"

Maya felt a fluttering in her stomach. "That's amazing!" she said. "I've always wanted to go on an adventure!"

Lottie and Rosalind smiled at each other. They knew they could trust these girls to keep their secret.

CHAPTER FOUR

The Ninja Plan

Maya ran downstairs to the kitchens and brought up tall glasses of lemonade with curly straws and bowls of ice cream with chocolate sauce on top. Then the four princesses talked excitedly about how they would go to see the snow leopards without anyone missing them!

Lottie amazed Maya and Summer with stories of the adventures they'd had as Rescue Princesses, especially the last one, when they'd rescued two tiger cubs.

Maya looked longingly at the jeweled rings on Rosalind's and Lottie's fingers. They'd told her they used these magic jewels to call one another when there was an animal rescue emergency.

Maya was also fascinated by *The Book of Ninja*. Its yellowy pages contained astonishing details about ninja moves and disguises. She felt like she could have read it forever, and she was disappointed when they were called down for lunch, followed by an afternoon of royal duties.

Maya woke early the next morning, full of excitement. She put on black leggings and a silver-gray T-shirt, picked up a bag with her finest royal dress and tiara inside, and crept downstairs. She stopped in the empty hallway, her heart racing as she thought of the plan they'd made yesterday. If this worked, they'd soon be on their way to the mountains to see the snow leopard cub!

"Maya!" hissed a voice. "We're over here."

Maya spotted a patch of curly red hair poking out from behind a pillar. "Hi, Lottie!" she called softly. "Are the others with you?"

"Yes, we're all here." Summer's smiling face peeked out from the other side. "We were just waiting for you."

Maya grinned. "Let's go, before the kings and queens wake up."

Lottie, Rosalind, and Summer darted out from behind the pillar. They were all wearing leggings and T-shirts, too, and carrying bags with their fancy clothes inside.

Maya led them outside. "Ready? We're going straight to the stables."

They ran across the garden, only slowing down once they'd turned the corner into the stable yard. There were five horses in the stalls, all busy eating hay. A chestnut-colored pony poked his head out to see what they were doing.

Maya collected the bags together and hid them in an empty stall. "As soon as we get back, we can change into our royal clothes, and no one will notice a thing."

"At last! We can go!" cried Rosalind. "But how are we going to get there? Isn't it too far to walk?"

Maya went over to her favorite pony, Dazzle, and rubbed his shiny black coat. "Yes, it's a pretty long way, and that's why I brought you to the stables. We're going to ride."

Rosalind turned pale. "But I don't know how to ride! Nobody said this was part of the plan."

"Don't worry, you can sit behind me. I'm a good rider," said Maya. "Lottie and Summer, can one of you ride a horse?"

"I can," said Summer. "I love horses."

"Me too!" Lottie's eyes gleamed. "We can take turns holding the reins."

"Take Fernleaf," said Maya, pointing to a small, sandy-colored pony. "She's very gentle."

"Hello, Fernleaf." Summer rubbed the pony's nose, and Fernleaf gave a soft answering whinny.

Maya handed out riding hats to everyone. Then she helped a nervous Rosalind onto Dazzle's back before getting on herself. Lottie and Summer climbed onto Fernleaf, and Lottie took the reins. Tapping her heels gently against Dazzle, Maya urged him forward. They trotted down the drive and through the palace gates.

"Are you all right, Rosalind?" asked Maya, turning to look behind her.

"I think so," said Rosalind. "It's a little bumpy, isn't it?"

Maya laughed. "I guess it is! Hold on tight because we're going to go faster!" She leaned forward to whisper in Dazzle's ear, and the little pony tossed his head and broke into a canter.

Fields rolled by as the horses gained speed, their hooves drumming on the ground and their tails flying. The city with the royal palace was now far behind them. Ahead rose a majestic row of mountains, all capped with glittering snow.

"It's really beautiful!" called Summer. "Which one is Ching-May Peak?"

"Ching-May is a small ridge halfway up the first mountain," Maya called back. "We're not far away now."

A few minutes later, Maya asked Dazzle to slow down. Then she leapt off, and Rosalind climbed down, too. "I really liked that!" said Rosalind, her cheeks pink. "I didn't know riding would be so much fun."

Maya smiled as she took off her riding hat. "Dazzle loves galloping, and he went just as fast as ever with two of us on his back." She led the pony over to a field with a fence around it. "We'll leave the ponies here. The farmer never minds us using this field."

The princesses said good-bye to Dazzle and Fernleaf and began the steep climb up the mountainside. The ground grew rockier and clumps of wildflowers pushed their way up between the stones. A low humming noise echoed around the mountains, and Maya wondered what it was.

"What a beautiful view," said Lottie. "Look, I can see the palace!"

But Maya didn't look at the view. She stopped climbing and frowned. "Do you hear that? There's a sort of chugging sound."

The noise got louder and the rocky ground shook. Some little pebbles rolled away down the mountainside.

"It sounds a little like a truck or a backhoe," said Summer.

Maya shook her head. "It can't be! No one is allowed to build anything on these mountains. This is a wildlife area by order of the king." She ran up the mountainside, her heart thudding.

"Slow down, Maya!" called Lottie.

Maya reached the smooth stone of Ching-May Peak and gazed down. Her heart sank. From here, she could see much more of the mountain. The lower slopes had been taken over by people in orange jackets and builders' helmets. They shouted to one another, motioning a huge backhoe forward. Two more trucks waited at the bottom. Part of the slope had already been flattened, and the rocks and wildflowers covered with dull brown earth.

The other girls caught up with her. "What is it, Maya?" Rosalind panted. "What's going on?"

Maya stared at the mountainside in horror. "They're not allowed to do that here! They must have started yesterday after I left. They've caused so much damage already."

"It does look like a real mess," said Lottie. "And I bet they've scared away the snow leopards."

Maya scanned the mountainside for any sign of the beautiful snow leopards. What if the little cub had been hurt?

Then she caught sight of something moving higher up on the slope. "There's the mother." She pointed. "But I can't see the cub."

"Where was their den?" asked Summer.

"I think it must have been among those rocks down there," said Maya. "It's hard to see because snow leopards choose places that are well hidden. I hope Cloudtail's gone with his mother."

Just then a furry white head peeked out of the rocks and looked around.

"There's the cub!" Rosalind pointed across the mountainside. "Poor little thing! Those machines must sound even louder over there."

"We have to help him." Maya's eyes shone with determination. "We have to tell those people to take their noisy equipment away."

CHAPTER FIVE

Backhoes on the Mountain

The princesses scrambled down the slope, the stones sliding beneath their feet. Maya went first because she knew the mountainside best. She took them down a path that skirted along a steep gully and led to where the builders were working.

"Stop!" cried Lottie over the noise of the backhoe. She waved her arms and the others joined in.

At last, one of the men saw them and

signaled to the person inside the digging machine, who shut off the engine.

"That's better," said Rosalind. "I can't stand that horrible noise, and goodness knows how scary it is for the cub!"

The first man marched over to them, looking angry. His orange jacket barely fit over his pudgy middle. "What do you think you're doing, little girls? You shouldn't be here."

"What?!" snapped Rosalind, but Lottie shushed her.

"This is a protected wildlife area," explained Maya. "Maybe you didn't know. No one is allowed to build here by order of the king."

"Is that right?" sneered the builder, turning to laugh with another man who'd just walked over. "And what would *you* four know about the king's orders?"

Maya felt her cheeks grow hot. "I know a lot about them, actually, because I'm Princess Maya, the king's daughter."

The men laughed even harder at this. "You don't look very royal to me," said the pudgy man. "Anyway, we have different royal orders to follow that you know nothing about. Now, off you go. We have a lot to get done today." He waved for the digger to start up again.

"But there's a snow leopard cub in a den over there!" cried Maya. But the men didn't hear her over the chugging noise of the machinery.

"How dare they not believe that we're royal!" Rosalind glared at the men.

"It's because we're not in our best dresses," said Maya. "Poor Cloudtail! He must be so frightened."

"We should rescue him," said Lottie. "Let's go get him from the den right now."

"I don't think we should," said Summer. "The machines aren't digging next to the den yet. There's a chance we could upset the mother snow leopard if we try to take the cub away. It's her instinct to protect her baby. It would be awful if she tried to come down here. The trucks and backhoes make it a dangerous place for an animal."

Maya glanced up at the mother snow leopard, who was still prowling across the higher slopes. "Deena, who works on the wildlife projects, is always telling me not to disturb a den." She bit her lip. "We need to get back home and tell my dad," she decided. "He'll be able stop these builders."

Lottie looked disappointed.

Together, they ran back to the field where their ponies were grazing. Dazzle and Fernleaf trotted over right away.

The girls put on their riding hats before climbing onto the ponies.

"Good boy!" Maya patted Dazzle's neck. "Take us home as quickly as you can."

The ponies set off at a fast pace. The wind streamed past the princesses' faces and made Summer's fair hair fly out behind her. Soon they left the fields behind and turned down the path that led through the huge stone archway into the palace garden.

Dazzle and Fernleaf sped into the stable yard, and the girls jumped down.

"Well done, Dazzle!" Maya rubbed the pony's shiny coat. Dazzle whinnied and trotted away to the water trough. Summer stroked Fernleaf, who bent her head to nuzzle the girl's shoulder.

"I've found our royal dresses!" Rosalind ran out of a stall holding the bags.

"There's no time to get changed!" cried Lottie.

"I think we should," said Maya. "Otherwise the grown-ups will get mad as soon as they see us."

The princesses picked up their clothes and each rushed into an empty stall to get changed. Maya came out first in a red-and-gold dress that stretched down to her ankles. She wore a heart-shaped tiara on top of her dark hair.

"I'm ready," she called, stuffing her T-shirt into her bag.

"Me too!" Lottie appeared in a crimson dress decorated with sparkly beads. A ruby tiara perched awkwardly on her red curls.

Summer rushed out in a yellow dress and a tiara made of flowers. "The poor snow leopard cub! I can't stop thinking about him in his den with all those machines roaring close by."

Maya, Summer, and Lottie looked back at the stall where Rosalind was still changing. "Come *on*, Rosy!" cried Lottie.

"All right! All right!" Rosalind hurried out, smoothing her dark blue dress and checking that her sapphire tiara was on straight.

They ran back through the garden, slowing down as they reached the front door. Maya hid the bags of clothes behind a large potted plant, and they headed straight into the banquet hall.

"There's no point using the ninja moves," said Lottie. "We want them to notice us."

Maya swallowed. "We'll just have to tell the truth about where we went. I don't mind if I get in trouble, as long as Cloudtail is safe from those backhoes."

They opened the door, expecting to hear a speech going on, but the kings and queens were talking over cups of coffee. Duke Levon was standing next to the throne, resting one hand on the Ice Diamond.

"So you're having a new palace built, are you?" Lottie's mom, the queen of Middingland, asked the duke politely.

"Oh yes! Once my palace is finished, it will be the biggest building in the whole kingdom," Duke Levon said loudly. "And it will have twenty stables, fifteen fountains, and seven swimming pools. My workmen are starting to build it today."

"Where's your dad, Maya?" asked Lottie. "I can't see him anywhere."

"I don't know." Maya looked around worriedly.

"Because there's no point settling for a tiny little palace," continued the duke. "Not when you're as royal as I am." His hand tightened on the diamond.

"Who *is* that?" hissed Summer.

"That's my uncle, Duke Levon," whispered Maya.

"I wonder what he's up to," said Summer quietly.

Maya's eyes widened as Summer went over to the duke and curtsied. "Excuse me," said Summer. "Could I ask you where this new palace will be?"

"Of course, young princess!" The duke smiled. "In fact, that's the other marvelous thing about it. My castle will stand on a mountainside. It will be the highest palace in the world!"

CHAPTER SIX

The Dastardly Duke

Maya gasped. Suddenly she understood why Summer had asked Duke Levon about his new palace. "But, Uncle!" she said to the duke. "Do you mean that you're having a palace built in the mountain wildlife area? Are the machines near Ching-May Peak there because of you?"

The duke fiddled with his black velvet robe. "What? No, of course not! It's a completely different mountain." He

58

glared at the princesses. "How do you know about those, anyway? You're supposed to have been here listening to the speeches and behaving yourselves."

He stared at Maya's feet. "Your shoes are dirty. You've been in the stables, haven't you? Did you go riding this morning?"

Lottie's eyes flashed. "We rode all the way to the mountain, and we saw exactly what was happening there. The hillside is being destroyed!"

The duke glared at her. "You nosy girl —" He broke off as King Ramesh walked in.

"Your Highnesses," said the king. "If you take your seats we'll carry on with the Grand Assembly."

All the kings and queens bustled around, finding their seats. Maya desperately tried to break through the crowd. "Dad!" she cried. "I've got something really important to tell you."

"Can it wait till afterward, please, Maya? We really must get on with the speeches." King Ramesh marched up to the throne and sat down. The Ice Diamond gleamed from the top of the throne.

"But it's an emergency," said Maya.

"There are backhoes on the mountainside," explained Rosalind. "We saw them this morning."

"And there's a snow leopard den nearby," added Summer.

"What's this?" The king's eyebrows rose. "You saw backhoes *this morning*?"

"I think I can explain, Brother," said Duke Levon smoothly. "These girls have been out riding this morning instead of doing their duty by attending this Assembly. You can see where they've been from the state of their hair and their clothes." Maya hurriedly picked some straw out of Lottie's tiara. "As soon as I discovered what they'd done, they invented this story about seeing backhoes on the mountain to cover up their terrible behavior."

"That's not true!" cried Rosalind.

"Dad! The snow leopards really could get hurt," said Maya. "We saw it all on Ching-May Peak."

"Nonsense!" King Ramesh looked stern. "Deena gave me a full report about the animals in that area yesterday and they were all perfectly fine." Maya tried to speak again but he held up his hand. "No more, please. I must say that I'm very disappointed in you. I told you that you should stay here and you ran off, anyway."

"Shocking behavior!" The duke

pretended to look indignant but Maya could see a faint smirk on his face.

"You clearly need some extra practice in good manners," continued the king. "Tomorrow you will sit with the kings and queens and practice talking politely and serving drinks and cake all morning."

"*All* morning!" said Maya.

"Yes, Maya," said King Ramesh. "Perhaps it will help you to remember that your royal duties are important." He looked at the other girls. "Actually, I will ask your parents if you can all join in. You can practice good manners together. Now, please sit down, I want to begin."

Downcast, Maya went to find a seat. She bit her lip. If only Deena hadn't gone to visit another wildlife area. Deena would have listened to what she was saying.

The other girls sat down next to her and Lottie muttered angrily, "It's that duke! *He* stopped us from explaining, and now the grown-ups will never listen!"

"It's because he ordered the diggers to start work," whispered Summer. "He doesn't want your dad to know about the new palace he's building, Maya."

Maya nodded. "He must be hoping that no one finds out and stops him. Then once the palace is finished, it'll be too late."

"We'll just have to find a way to stop those men and their machines ourselves," said Rosalind fiercely.

The princesses sat stiffly, waiting for the Grand Assembly to end. One speech followed another and another. Maya felt like they would never end. At last, King Ramesh thanked everyone and said it

was almost time for the banquet. Glad to be free, the girls ran right out of the hall and across the garden to the palace gates.

Two guards stepped in front of them. "I'm sorry, Princesses," said the tallest one. "We've been given strict orders by Duke Levon that no children should be allowed out of the palace gardens."

"But I've always been trusted to go out before," said Maya.

The guard shrugged. "Sorry, Princess Maya. We have to follow our orders."

Maya turned away from the guards, her eyes full of tears. "This is all my uncle's fault! Now what are we going to do?"

"At least the sun is setting," Summer pointed out. "So the men will have to stop work until tomorrow."

"But tomorrow morning they'll start up again. They'll destroy Cloudtail's home while I'm stuck inside talking politely to the royal guests all morning," said Maya.

"Why don't the grown-ups ever believe us?" said Rosalind gloomily.

"We have to find a way to prove that those builders really *are* digging at the bottom of the mountain," said Summer.

"If we took a photo we'd be able to show it to everyone," said Maya. "But how do we get out of here to do that?"

"By using *The Book of Ninja*!" said Rosalind, perking up.

The girls looked at one another. "We have to try something," said Maya. "The snow leopards need us."

Lottie nodded solemnly. "Rosalind and I made a promise to always help animals in trouble. Maya . . . Summer . . . will you join us and become Rescue Princesses, too?"

CHAPTER SEVEN

The Great Lizard Commotion

The princesses had to wait until the banquet was over to go to Rosalind's room and look at *The Book of Ninja* again.

"To be a Rescue Princess," Lottie said solemnly to Maya and Summer, "you must promise to help the snow leopards and other animals in danger, no matter how difficult it becomes."

Maya and Summer looked at each other. "We promise!" they said together.

"Good!" Lottie opened *The Book of*

Ninja. "There's no time to lose. Tomorrow morning we'll sneak out and take photos of the construction workers and all the damage they've done."

"We just need to find the right ninja move," said Rosalind, leaning over Lottie's shoulder. "Lottie, be careful! You'll crease the pages!"

"I *am* being careful," said Lottie, flipping on to the next page.

"The problem is that we need to escape from a hall full of kings and queens all expecting us to talk politely and serve them drinks," said Maya. "It'll take a pretty good ninja move to do that."

"What about using this one?" Rosalind pointed to a page that showed a ninja walking along a tightrope over a waterfall.

"I'm not sure we have any rope like that," said Maya, alarmed.

"How about we cause a distraction?" suggested Summer. "Then, while everyone's trying to see what's happening, we can sneak out the door."

"Great idea!" said Lottie excitedly. "And we could tell the guards that they're needed inside the palace, giving us the chance to get through the gate."

Rosalind sighed. "I suppose that's easier than the waterfall move. What could the distraction be?"

They were all silent for a moment, thinking. Maya caught a movement in the garden, as a dragon-eye lizard crawled over a stone. "I know!" she said. "I'll set a lizard free among the guests. They're lovely, gentle creatures, but they have a row of spikes on their heads and long tongues that can look scary. Sometimes they change color to match their surroundings."

"Ooh!" Rosalind shivered. "Lizards *are* sort of creepy. We don't have any in my country."

"That's settled, then," said Lottie. "Does anyone have a camera we can use?"

"I do," said Summer.

"I'll catch a lizard tomorrow morning and hide it in the hall," said Maya. "You could come and help me, Rosalind, and then you'll see that lizards are actually very nice!"

♥

Maya was pleased with the lizard plan and happy to be asked to become a member of the Rescue Princesses! But she couldn't stop worrying about Cloudtail. The little cub must be really frightened by the noise of the construction near his den. She couldn't believe this was all because her uncle wanted to build a huge palace.

She was glad when morning came and she could wake up Rosalind to help her catch a lizard. The two girls sneaked down to the garden to search for one of the creatures.

"They like to sleep in these gaps between the stones," said Maya, peering into a little hole. "Yes, here's one." She gently picked the lizard up and popped it into a small box with some air holes in the top.

"Can I touch the little guy?" Rosalind stroked it carefully. "It's scaly, but not as creepy as I thought."

The lizard turned its head and looked at her with a beady black eye.

"He likes you!" Maya smiled. Then she made sure the lizard was all right before she put the lid onto the box. "Come on, let's go and find him some vegetables to eat, and then we'll hide the box under one of the long tables in the hall."

The princesses met in the hall after breakfast, all wearing their best clothes and tiaras. Maya straightened her heart-shaped tiara and began setting cakes out on a silver tray. She needed to show she had good manners in front of all the royal guests. Then no one would suspect she was actually planning an escape! She glanced at Summer, who stood nearby setting out cups and saucers, and they both grinned.

King Ramesh walked in, talking to Lottie's mom and dad. He saw Maya and came over. "Excellent!" he said. "I'm pleased to see you looking after our guests. I have to go and make sure that everything's ready for the festival tomorrow. I hope you'll carry on the good work!"

"We will, Your Majesty!" said Summer, with a curtsy. After he left, she turned to Maya. "I don't see your uncle."

Maya glanced around. "You're right. He's not here. I wonder what he's up to."

She suddenly noticed something odd about the king's throne at the far side of the hall. The Ice Diamond at the top wasn't shining the way it usually did. It looked dull and pale.

Lottie came over. "Are you ready, Maya? Do you have the lizard?"

Maya stopped looking at the diamond. "He's hidden under a table. Just be ready to sneak out as soon as I release him."

Picking up the tray of cakes, she walked over to where several guests were seated. A long tablecloth hung down to the floor, hiding the underside of the table from view.

"Would you like a cake?" she asked the

kings and queens. "Oh, sorry! I think there's a stone in my shoe." Putting the tray on the table, she bent down and pretended to fiddle with her shoe. Instead, she put her hand under the long tablecloth and found the hidden box. She slipped the lizard out and watched it climb quickly up the tablecloth onto the table.

"Aaagh!" yelled a king with a beard. "What's that dangerous creature?"

The queen next to him gave a faint squeal and put her hand over her mouth.

"Oh no, it's a lizard!" said Maya loudly.

People sitting at other tables started to look around. "A lizard?" they repeated.

"Don't worry, Your Majesties!" shouted Lottie. "I'll get it!" She leaned toward the lizard, pretending to try to catch it.

The lizard ran over the cake tray and disappeared over the edge of the table,

darting down a table leg to reach the floor. Another queen shrieked. Maya knocked over a cup of tea to add to the general confusion. She noticed Lottie and Summer creeping quietly out of the door.

The lizard stopped on the ground and froze, changing color to match the brown floor.

"Oh no! What's happening to it?" yelped the king with the beard.

"Someone call the Lizard Catcher!" yelled Maya. "It's getting away!"

"Yes! Call the Lizard Catcher!" repeated the king.

Maya choked back a giggle. There *was* no Lizard Catcher, because the creatures weren't dangerous at all!

By now, kings and queens were rushing to and fro, trying to mop up spilled tea and keep an eye on the lizard. Some of

the younger princes and princesses
had run inside to find out what was
happening.

Maya looked at Rosalind and nodded.
It was time for the grand finale.

Taking a deep breath, Rosalind pointed
at the lizard and screeched, "The lizard is
coming to get me!" Then she toppled to
the floor, pretending that she was feeling
dizzy.

"Don't worry, Rosalind!" said Maya,
loudly. "I'll help you get some fresh air."

Taking the other girl's arm, she helped
her walk through the door. As they
passed the lizard, Maya managed to
scoop him up and take him with her.

As soon as they got outside, Maya
released the lizard into the garden. Then
she and Rosalind ran off to the stables,
giggling.

CHAPTER EIGHT

Cloudtail's Den

Maya ran into the stable yard with
Rosalind right behind her. Lottie and
Summer were waiting with the ponies.

"We told the guards they were needed
inside," said Lottie. "And they ran
straight to the palace."

"They'll go back to the gate once they
realize it's only a lizard," added Summer.
"So we'd better hurry."

Maya patted Dazzle's soft black coat.

"We don't even have time to change. It'll be funny riding in a dress."

They left their tiaras in an empty stall and put on riding hats. Then they climbed onto the ponies and rode quickly toward the palace gate. Maya could feel Rosalind holding tight to her waist. She leaned down to whisper in Dazzle's ear. "Go as fast as you can!"

The pony tossed his mane and sped up. The palace gates passed in a blur, and they raced on into the countryside. Fernleaf galloped beside them with Lottie and Summer on her back.

At last, they came to the foot of the mountain and slowed down. Maya jumped off and helped Rosalind climb down from Dazzle's back. The grumbling sound of construction was louder than before. They could hear the machines before they'd even finished putting the ponies into their field.

The princesses ran across the slope toward the curve of the mountain, where they would be able to see the machines and the snow leopard's den. They gazed around anxiously.

"I'll take some pictures." Summer picked up the camera, which hung on a strap around her neck.

"Look, Maya!" Lottie pointed. "Isn't that your uncle?"

Duke Levon was standing on a stretch of flattened ground, talking to the pudgy builder that the girls had met the day before. The duke grinned widely as he spoke, and pointed to the dull brown earth covering the mountainside.

"Yes, that's him," said Maya. "And look, there's Cloudtail, peeking out of his den. I hoped he might have escaped up the mountain by now."

The girls gazed at Cloudtail. His head was poking out from a gap in the rocks. They could just see his gray-white ears and a pair of blue, inquisitive eyes. Suddenly, he popped his head farther out and mewed unhappily.

"Poor thing!" said Summer as she began taking photos. "He must be really hungry and want his mother, but she's probably too wary of the backhoes to come back to the den."

"What's that in Duke Levon's hand?" asked Rosalind.

The duke had taken something out of his pocket. It was round, and it sparkled brightly in the sunlight. Maya knew what it was right away. "That's the Ice Diamond! My uncle must have stolen it from the top of the throne. I can't believe he would do that." She remembered how dull and strange the diamond had looked earlier that morning. Her uncle must have already taken the real diamond and left a fake one in its place!

"Let's get closer and try to hear what they're saying," said Lottie.

The princesses crept a little farther up the mountainside.

"The palace will take a long time to build," the workman was saying.

"Hurry up, then!" replied the duke. "I don't want to wait weeks for it to be ready. I want it done quickly. Then I can put a fabulous throne inside with this diamond at the top."

"I promise that we're working as fast as we can," said the builder, and he bowed before climbing into his backhoe and turning on the engine.

It rumbled across the mountainside and dug its big metal teeth into the earth.

"The backhoe's getting too close to the cub's den!" Lottie shouted over the noise. "There's no time to take the photos back to the palace. We have to stop this right now."

"You're right!" called Summer. "Let's go!"

The princesses ran forward just as the backhoe dropped its scooped-up earth into a pile and swung around to dig again. This time the metal teeth got stuck in a rock. The ground shook, and the machine roared wildly.

"Stop!" yelled Summer, waving her arms at the builder.

The others joined in.

"Stop digging!" shouted Lottie.

"You're too close to the snow leopard's den," cried Maya.

The duke saw them, and his face turned red. The man inside the machine was still trying to pull the vehicle's shovel out of the ground. He pushed the levers hard, and at last, the shovel came out, pulling the rock loose with it. The mountainside shuddered, and the stones around the cub's den crumbled.

"Cloudtail!" cried Maya, dashing toward the den.

The builder turned off the machine's engine and climbed out. Then he walked over to look at the crumbled rocks.

"What are *you* doing here?" The duke snapped at the girls. "How dare you follow me!" The huge diamond gleamed in his hand.

"We couldn't stay away while the snow leopards were in danger," said Maya. "Uncle, there's a little cub living in a den among those rocks. We have to see if he's hurt."

The driver of the vehicle turned around and saw the girls, and his mouth dropped open. He called to a worker who was unloading cement bags from a truck.

Both men came over to Maya and bowed. "Your Majesty! It *was* you all the time. We're sorry we didn't recognize you yesterday in those different clothes."

Maya glanced at her royal dress. "I understand. But no one's allowed to dig in the wildlife area. There's a snow leopard den nearby."

The round-faced builder looked surprised. "The duke told us that the king had given special permission for the building of a new palace. Isn't that true?"

Duke Levon's eyes narrowed, and he hid the Ice Diamond behind his back.

"I didn't say the king had given his permission *exactly*. . . ."

"The king would *never* let anyone build here!" cried Maya. "Quickly! Help me look for the snow leopard cub."

"Of course, Princess Maya." The men bowed again. "We'll help you right away."

"You will *not*!" Duke Levon stamped his foot. "You work for me. Now get back into that machine."

"I'm sorry, Duke Levon," said the other builder. "But I don't think you told us the truth. Show us where this den is, Princess Maya."

Maya ran past the construction vehicles with Summer, Lottie, and the builders following her. They all scrambled across the gray rocks.

"This is outrageous! I'm fetching the guards." The duke stormed off, but he'd only gone a few steps when Rosalind got in his way. She bumped into him, making him stagger backward.

"Oh! Sorry about that," said Rosalind, not looking very sorry.

The duke muttered darkly and continued down the slope. At the bottom, he got into a large black car and drove off. Rosalind watched him go, then she bent down to pick something up from the ground.

Maya's heart was pounding as she stumbled over the rough mountainside. The rocks had crumbled so much that she was afraid she might not be able to find the den. What if Cloudtail had been hurt by the rockfall?

"I found him," called Summer, pointing to a gap in the earth.

Maya knelt down by the crack and looked into the darkness. The other girls crowded behind her. All they could see was a small white shape at the bottom. Cloudtail pawed at the sides of the hole, mewing sadly.

"The machines must have weakened the ground and made the den into a much deeper hole, Your Majesty," said the round-faced builder.

Maya looked at Cloudtail at the bottom of the chasm and a lump came to her throat. "Don't worry, Cloudtail. We'll get you out of there," she called down to the cub.

Poor Cloudtail just gave a sad little mew in reply.

CHAPTER NINE

The Crack in the Ground

"What would you like us to do, Your Majesties?" asked the second builder. "If we try to dig the cub out we could shake the ground even more and make things worse."

"You've caused a lot of damage already!" snapped Rosalind.

"Find the nearest farmer who can lend us some rope," Lottie told the men. "We're getting that little cub out no matter what."

"And please tell the other builders to turn off their machines," added Maya.

The men hurried away.

"Look, that must be the cub's mother." Summer pointed to a snow leopard much higher up the mountain.

"I wish this hole wasn't so narrow," said Maya. "Even with the rope, I don't think those men will be able to climb down here." She stretched her arm into the hole, but Cloudtail was still a long way out of reach.

The ground trembled, making Summer grab hold of Lottie.

"I'm going down there myself," decided Maya.

"You can't!" said Lottie. "The earth is still moving. You could get stuck down there, too!"

"I have to! The cub's all alone," said Maya.

"Maybe we can use this to help us?" Rosalind opened her hand to show the others the Ice Diamond.

"Where did you get that?" gasped Maya.

"I bumped into your uncle on purpose as he was leaving. He dropped the jewel, just like I hoped he would, and he was in too much of a hurry to notice," said Rosalind.

"Nice ninja moves, Rosalind!" said Summer.

"Thanks!" Rosalind smiled. "You said there was a story about this diamond, Maya. What is it?"

Maya stared at the clear jewel that glittered brightly in Rosalind's hand. "The diamond is supposed to provide great strength — that's how the legend goes. The first king of Lepari is said to have used it to build the kingdom."

"Can a jewel really make you strong?" Summer asked doubtfully.

"We've used magic jewels before," said Rosalind. "Haven't we, Lottie?"

Lottie nodded. "Lots of times, and if this diamond is supposed to make people strong, then it could definitely help us."

Summer leaned forward to touch the jewel's sparkling surface. "I don't feel any different."

"Maybe you actually have to be holding it to get the extra strength," said Rosalind.

Suddenly, Cloudtail began mewing frantically and scraping at the sides of the hole.

"I'm going down there now," said Maya. "Then at least I can keep him calm until help comes." Carefully, she swung her legs into the hole.

Holding on to the edge, she searched

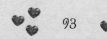

for a jutting-out rock that would help her to climb down. But the stones lining the hole were loose, and they slipped away beneath her feet. She plunged down. Her arms scraped against the sharp rocks, and she hoped desperately that Cloudtail would stay out of the way. She didn't want to hurt him!

Hitting the bottom, she fell sideways and grazed her right arm even more. Clutching her elbow, she looked around for the cub. He was crouching on the opposite side of the hole, shivering.

"It's all right, Cloudtail," said Maya, breathlessly. "I've come to help you."

Cloudtail mewed back at her as if he was talking. He stopped shivering and took a careful step toward Maya.

"That's it, come on," she said encouragingly, and held out her hand.

The cub crept a little closer and sniffed

her fingers, his tail swaying uncertainly. Then he looked up at her with his beautiful blue eyes and mewed again.

"Come here." Maya gently lifted him up and hugged him. "We'll find a way out of here, don't worry." She stroked his head, feeling his soft fur.

The cub pricked up his ears and licked her hand with his little pink tongue.

"Are you all right, Maya?" called Summer.

Maya looked up and saw the princesses' faces at the top. From down here, the hole seemed even narrower. Her heart beat faster. She didn't like feeling trapped, especially when she knew the ground was unsteady. "Yes, I'm all right, and Cloudtail's fine, too," she managed to say.

"How far can you reach?" asked Lottie.

Maya reached up with one arm while holding Cloudtail tight with the other.

Even on tiptoe, she could only stretch halfway to the top of the hole.

"Just wait a minute," said Summer. "We've got an idea."

There was movement at the top, and then Summer lay down, stretching her torso and shoulders down into the hole.

"Stop, Summer!" Maya cried in alarm. "You'll fall in headfirst."

"Don't worry. Lottie's holding on to my ankles so that I don't fall in, and Rosalind is holding on to hers." Summer's face started turning red. "If the Ice Diamond really *can* make people stronger then Rosalind will be able to pull us all up. Quick! Take my hand."

Maya tried to reach Summer's fingers but couldn't stretch high enough. Keeping Cloudtail safe with one arm, she climbed onto a small ledge. This time, she grabbed the other girl's hand easily.

"Now, Rosalind! Pull!" shouted Summer, gripping Maya's hand tightly.

At once, Maya felt herself being pulled off her feet. She and Cloudtail dangled in the air, gradually rising higher. The cub mewed excitedly and lifted his nose toward the sunlight at the top of the hole.

"Ow! This is hurting my arm," groaned Summer.

"I can pull faster!" called Rosalind. "It's like being a superpowered princess!"

Maya felt herself rising even more quickly. Her head reached the top of the hole, and she gently set Cloudtail down before pulling herself onto the rocks at the edge.

"That was the strangest thing I've ever done!" said Summer, getting up. "And my clothes have gotten torn on the rocks. But it doesn't matter, because you're safe now!" She stroked Cloudtail's beautiful fur and he nuzzled her hand.

"He's adorable," said Lottie. "Look at how thick his fur is."

Suddenly, Cloudtail raised his nose, as if he'd caught a scent from higher up the mountain. His eyes brightened.

"Aw! I bet he can tell that his mother's close by," said Lottie.

"We should try to get him back to his mom right away." Summer glanced at the higher slopes, looking for the mother snow leopard.

"Let's take Cloudtail a little farther up the mountain and see if we can spot her." Maya looked at the Ice Diamond glittering in Rosalind's hand. "Thank goodness you had the idea to use the jewel, Rosalind, and it's so awesome that the stories about it are true." She reached out to touch the gem, still amazed that it had such power.

"You get used to awesomeness when you're a Rescue Princess." Rosalind grinned. "And you've just had your first adventure!"

CHAPTER TEN

The Missing Diamond

The princesses carried Cloudtail up the mountain. They left the bare earth and construction behind, climbing up a slope dotted with wildflowers.

"I can see the mother snow leopard — over there behind that tall grass," said Summer.

"Then we'd better not go any closer." Maya put the cub down and gave him one last pet.

"Good-bye, Cloudtail," said Lottie.

Cloudtail mewed, his long tail waving excitedly. The mother snow leopard padded closer, and the girls hurried away down the slope. Then they watched from a distance as the cub skipped up to his mother and wound between her legs.

She leaned over to nuzzle his ears and lick his face. When she'd finished washing him, she set off up the mountainside.

Cloudtail looked back at Maya for a moment and pricked up his ears before he scampered over the grass behind his mother.

"They should be safe for now," said Maya. "But we need to make sure my uncle gives up his palace-building plans."

Just then, the two builders rushed toward them carrying a long coil of rope. "We found this, Your Majesties," they called.

"Oh, we don't need *that* anymore," said Lottie. "You can take it away again."

"Wait!" said Maya. "Before you go, you have to move these machines away from here." She pointed to the backhoe and trucks. "You must also promise never to disturb the snow leopards again."

"We promise, Your Majesty," they replied. "And we're really sorry," added the round-faced man.

Maya smiled and turned to the other princesses. "In a few weeks, new plants will grow in this earth, and the whole mountainside will look beautiful again."

♥

The princesses enjoyed riding Dazzle and Fernleaf back to the palace. It was a fresh spring morning and butterflies rose from the meadows and fluttered past them into the air. There were no guards at the palace gate, so they trotted the ponies right to the stables.

"We'll have to explain what happened to my dad and give him back the Ice Diamond," said Maya, taking off her riding hat and patting Dazzle.

"It's too bad we can't keep it." Rosalind gazed at the twinkling diamond. "I liked being super strong. It was really handy!"

"I think my dad will want the jewel to go back on the throne," said Maya, laughing.

They left the ponies with food and fresh water, and walked across the garden to the palace. The hall was crowded with kings and queens all talking anxiously.

"What's the matter? Why's everyone looking so worried?" Lottie asked a young prince.

"Someone stole the king's enormous diamond and put a fake one in its place," he replied. "It's really exciting! I hope the robber gets arrested."

Maya looked through the crowd. Her dad, King Ramesh, was standing next to the throne, frowning deeply. The fake diamond at the top looked dull and strange, just as it had that morning.

"It's all right!" said Lottie. "We can tell the king that the jewel is safe."

Just then Maya noticed Duke Levon sitting near the king. The duke saw her at the same moment and sprang to his feet, walking straight over to his brother. "There they are!" He pointed at the girls. "*They* took the Ice Diamond. I saw them carrying it, and I followed them to try and take it back."

"Hey!" said Rosalind. "That isn't what happened."

"Search them!" shouted the duke. "Look in their pockets. You're sure to find the jewel."

"There's no need." Maya took the jewel

from Rosalind, who was frowning at the duke. She held it up in the air. "We didn't take the diamond in the first place. We just found it and brought it back."

She felt herself turning red. Some of the kings and queens had begun murmuring to one another. Many of them looked very disapproving.

Lottie's mom pushed through the crowd. "Lottie, what on earth is going on? You look so dirty and you've torn your best dress."

"It's all right, Mom. *We* didn't take the jewel," said Lottie. "We found it when we went to stop the duke from hurting the snow leopards."

"That's a very serious thing to say," said King Ramesh.

"I'm afraid they're mad at me because I saw through their silly story," scoffed the duke.

"Actually, we can prove that there was construction near a snow leopard den. We can prove that Duke Levon was there, too," Summer said firmly. "I took some pictures on my camera." She took the camera from around her neck and went through the crowd to give it to the king.

Duke Levon's eyebrows rose and he started to edge away. "I really must . . . I mean, I can't possibly stay . . ."

"This is terrible! What a dreadful sight!" King Ramesh stared at the pictures, then he looked up at the duke. "Brother, you're standing right in the middle of the damaged mountainside and holding the Ice Diamond in your hand. Tell me right now, in front of my guests, why were you destroying the wildlife area?"

Duke Levon glared down his nose. "*My* guests!" he growled. "It's always *my* guests, *my* diamond, and *my* throne, isn't it? When are you going to give something to *me*?"

"He was trying to build a palace on the mountainside," said Maya. "He was talking about it yesterday."

Several kings and queens in the crowd murmured in agreement.

"I'm very disappointed to hear that," said the king.

"But I *need* a large palace," cried Duke Levon. "Who cares about the snow leopards, anyway?"

"Everyone in Lepari cares about them except you, it seems." The king frowned. "You are banished from this palace. Guards, take the duke away."

The guards marched Duke Levon from the room.

"Come here, please, Maya," said the king.

Maya went to the front and handed the Ice Diamond to her father. "Dad, I know you wanted me to stay here but there was a snow leopard cub up there. I named him Cloudtail. His home was going to be destroyed, and I couldn't leave him in danger!" she said all in one breath.

"I'm glad you care so much about the snow leopards, Maya," said King Ramesh. "I should have listened to you. As a reward for your brave actions, you and your new friends will be in the parade tomorrow. You can ride in the first carriage."

"Really?" Maya's eyes lit up. "Can we throw candy into the crowd and everything?"

King Ramesh smiled. "You can throw candy and everything!"

CHAPTER ELEVEN

The Lepari Spring Festival

Maya was bursting with excitement the next morning. The Spring Festival happened every year, but she didn't usually take part in the parade. Riding in the very first carriage was going to be the best thing *ever*!

She put on a yellow dress with glittery buttons. Then she brushed her hair and braided it again, and put on her heart-shaped tiara. Lastly, she added her favorite gold necklace. She thought of Cloudtail. He would be high on the mountainside with his mother. Maybe they had made a new den already!

"Maya!" Lottie rushed into the room without knocking. "Are you ready? Your dad says our carriage is waiting."

"I'm ready!" Maya followed Lottie downstairs. Summer and Rosalind were standing on the steps outside.

"Have a wonderful time, girls," said King Ramesh.

"Thank you! We will!" The princesses climbed into the golden carriage and sat down on the plump red cushions. The coachman spoke and the carriage rolled forward, pulled by four white horses with gleaming bridles.

"Here's the candy that we throw to the crowd," said Maya, handing out bags filled with little chocolates and hard candies. "As soon as we reach the city streets, you'll see everyone waving and cheering."

Rosalind peered into her bag. "But we don't have to throw all of these, right? I want to eat some, too."

Maya grinned. "That's OK. I don't think anyone will mind."

"That's good! I've already eaten five of mine!" said Summer. "I'm so glad I met you all. Hey! Why don't I ask my mom and dad if you can all come and stay at my palace in Mirrania? Then I can show you our amazing animals. I even have a pet parrot called Kanga!"

"I'd love to come to Mirrania," said Maya, beaming. "I hope your parents like the idea."

"But even when we're far apart we can still talk to each other." Lottie nudged Rosalind. "Can't we? Are you listening to me, Rosy?"

"All right! I didn't forget." Rosalind put down her bag of candy and reached into her pocket. "Last night we talked to Amina and Isabella, the other two girls that became Rescue Princesses with us. They were sad that they couldn't be here, but they're really happy that you're both joining the Rescue Princess gang!"

Maya suddenly remembered how the girls spoke to one another when they were apart. "You must have used your magic rings to talk to them. I wish I'd seen that!" She looked at the heart-shaped rings on their fingers.

"Yes, but that's the thing!" Lottie burst out.

"Shhh! You said I could tell them," said Rosalind.

"Go ahead, then!" Lottie bounced on the seat in excitement.

"Well, you see . . . we have a jewel-crafting kit and some spare jewels. So we made you magic rings, too!"

Rosalind took her hand out of her pocket and showed them two more heart-shaped rings. One had a purple amethyst jewel, and the other was made from a lovely green aquamarine.

"So now we can talk to you using the rings, too, and if an animal's in danger, we can call you right away," said Lottie, beaming.

"They look awesome!" Summer picked up the purple ring and put it on.

"Thank you!" cried Maya, taking the pale green ring. She slid it onto her finger and admired the beautiful aquamarine jewel. It reminded her of the color of the meadows at the bottom of the mountain.

"Rescue Princesses forever!" said Lottie, holding out her hand with the ruby ring.

"Forever!" echoed the other girls, putting their hands on top of hers.

As their hands joined, the four heart-shaped jewels lit up brightly for a moment. Maya and Summer gasped.

"Wow!" said Maya. "Did you know the rings would do that?"

"Of course! That's the power of the jewels," explained Rosalind.

The carriage turned a corner into a wide street, and the girls could hear the cheering of the crowd ahead. They picked up their bags of candy, ready to throw them to the waiting people.

Maya grinned at her friends as she took a handful of candies. Having more adventures as a Rescue Princess would be a dream come true!

Can't wait for
the Rescue Princesses' next
daring animal adventure?

The Rainbow Opal

Turn the page for
a sneak peek!

CHAPTER ONE

Exploring the Woods

Princess Summer raced downstairs, her golden hair bouncing on her shoulders. She knew her friends were waiting for her outside. Jumping down the last two steps, she ran toward the door.

Summer's mom, the queen of Mirrania, came into the hallway. "Wait a minute, Summer! Where are you going?"

"I'm taking my friends to the woods to show them all the animals," said Summer.

"What about your hair?" said the queen. "Have you brushed it?"

"I think I did." Summer flicked back her hair. "I'm sure it looks all right, anyway."

The queen sighed. "Well, don't forget that the photographer's coming today."

"I won't. See you later!" Summer rushed out of the door.

The sun beat down on the walls and pointed towers of the palace. Straight ahead lay a neat garden full of bright flowers, with the wild forest just beyond.

Three princesses were waiting for Summer at the bottom of the palace steps. Maya was smiling shyly, her dark braid hanging over her shoulder. Lottie was practicing cartwheels on the grass. Rosalind stood with her arms folded, tapping her foot impatiently.

Summer's heart lifted as she ran toward them. She'd met the girls when she'd visited Maya's palace in the kingdom of Lepari. They had climbed a steep mountain to rescue a snow leopard cub from terrible danger. It had been an amazing adventure!

Lottie and Rosalind had explained that they'd set up a secret club for rescuing animals, and it was called the Rescue Princesses. She'd felt so happy when they'd asked her to join. She loved animals and always wanted to help them. Now she had friends that felt that way, too!

Each Rescue Princess wore a ring with a magical jewel. The jewels let them call one another when they found an animal in trouble. Summer's jewel was a beautiful purple amethyst. She touched it and smiled.

Lottie stopped cartwheeling and looked at Summer. The breeze ruffled her curly red hair. "We're all ready, Summer! What did you want to show us?"

"Lots of things!" replied Summer. "There's a whole forest full of animals and birds beyond that gate." She pointed to an old wooden gate in the corner. "It was dark when you all arrived yesterday, so I couldn't show it to you. But I know you'll like it. We have amazing animals here in Mirrania. There are kangaroos, possums, and koalas, and in the evening, you can see bats flying around."

"Awesome!" said Lottie.

"Oh, I almost forgot! First of all, you have to meet Kanga." Summer gazed around the garden, calling out, "Kanga? Where are you?"